WHAT'S IN MY LUNCHBOX?

For Mum – thanks for packing my lunch for all those years. PC

For darling Coco & Babette, may you find only good surprises in your lunchboxes! KC

First published in Australia 2015
This edition first published in 2020 by New Frontier Publishing Europe Ltd
Uncommon, 126 New King's Rd, London SW6 4LZ
www.newfrontierpublishing.co.uk

Text copyright © Peter Carnavas, 2015 • Illustrations copyright © Kat Chadwick, 2015

A CIP catalogue record for this book
is available from the British Library.
ISBN: 978-1-912858-56-9

Designed by Celeste Hulme
Printed in China
1 3 5 7 9 10 8 6 4 2

WHAT'S IN MY LUNCHBOX?

Peter Carnavas   Kat Chadwick

Today in my lunchbox
I happened to find …

an APPLE.

I don't like apples.

Today in my lunchbox
I happened to find ...

a FISH.
I don't like fish.

Today in my lunchbox
I happened to find ...

an EGG.
I don't like eggs.

Today in my lunchbox
I happened to find ...

a BEAR!
I don't like bears.

Today in my lunchbox
I happened to find ...

a
DINOSAUR!
I really don't like dinosaurs.

Today in my lunchbox
I happened to find ...

MY SISTER? NOT MY SISTER!

Today in my lunchbox
I happened to find ...

an APPLE.

I think I like apples.